For Esme,
my little one, giggle one, happy in the middle one.
Love, Granna
—B. J.

To my nieces, Somin and Jungmin —H. Y.

VIKING
Published by the Penguin Group
Penguin Young Readers Group, 345 Hudson Street, New York, New York 10014, U.S.A.
Penguin Group (Canada), 90 Eglinton Avenue East, Suite 700, Toronto, Ontario,
Canada M4P 2Y3 (a division of Pearson Penguin Canada Inc.)
Penguin Books Ltd, 80 Strand, London WC2R 0RL, England
Penguin Ireland, 25 St Stephen's Green, Dublin 2, Ireland (a division of Penguin Books Ltd)
Penguin Group (Australia), 250 Camberwell Road, Camberwell, Victoria 3124,
Australia (a division of Pearson Australia Group Pty Ltd)
Penguin Books India Pvt Ltd, 11 Community Centre, Panchsheel Park, New Delhi – 110 017, India
Penguin Group (NZ), 67 Apollo Drive, Rosedale, Auckland 0632, New Zealand (a division of Pearson New Zealand Ltd.)
Penguin Books (South Africa) (Pty) Ltd, 24 Sturdee Avenue, Rosebank, Johannesburg 2196, South Africa

Penguin Books Ltd, Registered Offices: 80 Strand, London WC2R 0RL, England

First published in the United States of America by Viking, an imprint of Penguin Young Readers Group, 2013

1   3   5   7   9   10   8   6   4   2

Text copyright © Barbara Joosse, 2013
Illustrations copyright © Hyewon Yum, 2013
All rights reserved

LIBRARY OF CONGRESS CATALOGING-IN-PUBLICATION DATA
Joosse, Barbara M.
Hooray Parade / by Barbara Joosse; illustrated by Hyewon Yum.
p. cm.
Summary: "Using the window as her stage, Gramma uses the things in her basket to create a wonderful parade of
shadow animals."—Provided by publisher.
ISBN 978-0-670-01334-0 (hardcover)
[1. Stories in rhyme. 2. Puppet theater—Fiction. 3. Grandmothers—Fiction.] I. Yum, Hyewon, ill. II. Title.
PZ8.3.J756Hoo 2013   [E]—dc23   2012028655

Manufactured in China   Set in Generis Serif Com
The artwork for this book was rendered in watercolor and linoleum block prints.

ALWAYS LEARNING   PEARSON

Hooray Parade

by **Barbara Joosse**   illustrated by **Hyewon Yum**

Viking
An Imprint of Penguin Group (USA) Inc.

Hooray!

Someone's coming to play with you.
Can you guess who?

Gramma!

Goodie goodie Gramma in a pink bandana
slicing up banana cake
banana cake that Gramma made
a piece for you, a piece for me
banana cake for you and me.

Thank you, Gramma.

Something's hiding in Gramma's basket.
Can you guess what's inside?

A Hooray Parade!

A Hooray Parade for
your windowsill
my little one, giggle one
happy in the middle one.

Hip-hip HOORAY!

Gallump gallump.
Can you guess what's coming up?

Elephant!

Elephant with a stripy trunk
a pink and purple stripy trunk
snorting out red confetti
ready ready red confetti!

WHEEEE!

Something's leaping from a tree.
Can you guess what's coming next?

Monkey!

Monkey's leaping from a tree
hopping, tumbling from a tree.

Tee hee hee. Tee hee hee.
Oh tiny straw hat, oh tiny tin drum
a-ratting and a-tatting on his
tiny tin drum.

Funny monkey!

Something's bobbing in the sky.
Can you guess what's coming next?

Rhinoceri!

Rhinoceri are bobbing by
orange balloons on their fingers
orange balloons on their toeses
orange balloons on the horns
  on top of their noses
balloony here, balloony there
balloony rhinos everywhere.

Let's blow kisses to the rhinos.

Fancy that!
Can you guess what's coming next?

Ostrich!

Ostrich in a party hat

dingle-dangle diamonds on her back
tinkle-tankle rubies on her toes
kicking up her fancy feet—
dingle dangle twinkle toes.

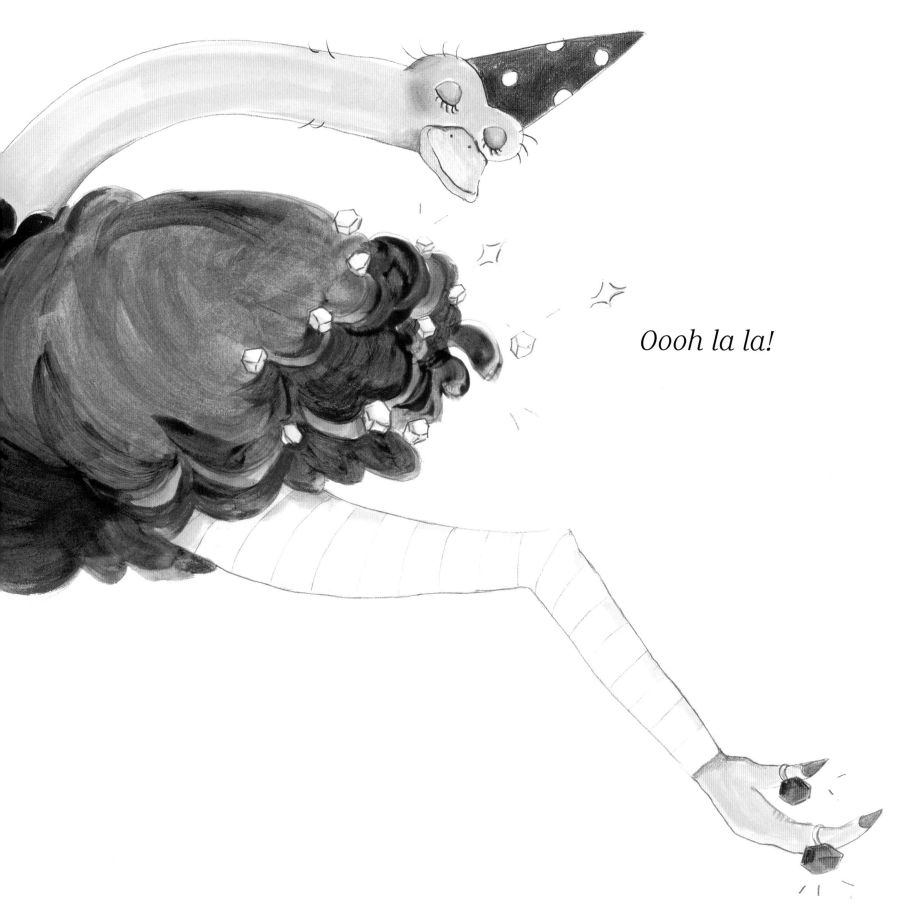

Oooh la la!

Now it's time for the Grand Finale.
Can you guess what's coming last?

Kangaroo!

Kangaroo with her joey inside
jumpy jumpy joey inside
a-rooting and a-tooting their blue kazoos—
the kangaroo kazoo caboose.

THE END!

No no, Gramma, that's not *the end.*

Something's missing. Something good.
Someone big and someone little.
Can *you* guess what's coming next?

Gramma and me!

Goodie goodie Gramma and me
marching in our clownie suits
honky-tonky clownie suits
stars of the Hooray Parade.

Hooray!